John G. Whittier

Snow-Bound and Among the Hills

John G. Whittier

Snow-Bound and Among the Hills

ISBN/EAN: 9783337256999

Printed in Europe, USA, Canada, Australia, Japan

Cover: Foto ©Andreas Hilbeck / pixelio.de

More available books at **www.hansebooks.com**

SNOW-BOUND

AND

AMONG THE HILLS

BY

JOHN G. WHITTIER

WITH EXPLANATORY NOTES

BOSTON
HOUGHTON, MIFFLIN AND COMPANY
New York : 11 East Seventeenth Street
The Riverside Press, Cambridge
1883

The Riverside Press, Cambridge:
Electrotyped and Printed by H. O. Houghton & Co.

I.

SNOW-BOUND.

A WINTER IDYL.

"As the Spirits of Darkness be stronger in the dark, so good Spirits
which be Angels of Light are augmented not only by the Divine light of the
Sun, but also by our common VVood Fire : and as the Celestial Fire drives
away dark spirits, so also this our Fire of VVood doth the same." — COR.
AGRIPPA, *Occult Philosophy*, Book I. ch v.

> "Announced by all the trumpets of the sky,
> Arrives the snow ; and, driving o'er the fields,
> Seems nowhere to alight ; the whited air
> Hides hills and woods, the river and the heaven,
> And veils the farm-house at the garden's end.
> The sled and traveller stopped, the courier's feet
> Delayed, all friends shut out, the housemates sit
> Around the radiant fireplace, inclosed
> In a tumultuous privacy of storm."
>
> EMERSON, *The Snow-Storm.*

THE sun that brief December day
Rose cheerless over hills of gray,
And, darkly circled, gave at noon
A sadder light than waning moon.
5 Slow tracing down the thickening sky
Its mute and ominous prophecy,
A portent seeming less than threat,
It sank from sight before it set.
A chill no coat, however stout,
10 Of homespun stuff could quite shut out,
A hard, dull bitterness of cold,
That checked, mid-vein, the circling race

Of life-blood in the sharpened face,
The coming of the snow-storm told.
15 The wind blew east; we heard the roar
Of Ocean on his wintry shore,
And felt the strong pulse throbbing there
Beat with low rhythm our inland air.

Meanwhile we did our nightly chores, —
20 Brought in the wood from out of doors,
Littered the stalls, and from the mows
Raked down the herd's-grass for the cows:
Heard the horse whinnying for his corn;
And, sharply clashing horn on horn,
25 Impatient down the stanchion rows
The cattle shake their walnut bows;
While, peering from his early perch
Upon the scaffold's pole of birch,
The cock his crested helmet bent
30 And down his querulous challenge sent.
Unwarmed by any sunset light
The gray day darkened into night.
A night made hoary with the swarm
And whirl-dance of the blinding storm.
35 As zigzag wavering to and fro
Crossed and recrossed the wingéd snow:
And ere the early bedtime came
The white drift piled the window-frame,
And through the glass the clothes-line posts
40 Looked in like tall and sheeted ghosts.

So all night long the storm roared on:
The morning broke without a sun:
In tiny spherule traced with lines

Of Nature's geometric signs,
45 In starry flake and pellicle
All day the hoary meteor fell;
And, when the second morning shone,
We looked upon a world unknown,
On nothing we could call our own.
50 Around the glistening wonder bent
The blue walls of the firmament.
No cloud above, no earth below, —
A universe of sky and snow!
The old familiar sights of ours
55 Took marvellous shapes; strange domes and towers
Rose up where sty or corn-crib stood,
Or garden-wall, or belt of wood;
A smooth white mound the brush-pile showed,
A fenceless drift what once was road;
60 The bridle-post an old man sat
With loose-flung coat and high cocked hat;
The well-curb had a Chinese roof;
And even the long sweep, high aloof,
In its slant splendor, seemed to tell
65 Of Pisa's leaning miracle.

A prompt, decisive man, no breath
Our father wasted: " Boys, a path! "
Well pleased, (for when did farmer boy
Count such a summons less than joy?)

65. The Leaning Tower of Pisa, in Italy, which inclines from the perpendicular a little more than six feet in eighty, is a campanile, or bell-tower, built of white marble, very beautiful, but so famous for its singular deflection from perpendicularity as to be known almost wholly as a curiosity. Opinions differ as to the leaning being the result of accident or design, but the better judgment makes it an effect of the character of the soil on which it is built. The Cathedral to which it belongs has suffered so much from a similar cause that there is not a vertical line in it.

70 Our buskins on our feet we drew;
    With mittened hands, and caps drawn low,
    To guard our necks and ears from snow,
    We cut the solid whiteness through.
    And, where the drift was deepest, made
75 A tunnel walled and overlaid
    With dazzling crystal : we had read
    Of rare Aladdin's wondrous cave,
    And to our own his name we gave,
    With many a wish the luck were ours
80 To test his lamp's supernal powers.
    We reached the barn with merry din,
    And roused the prisoned brutes within.
    The old horse thrust his long head out,
    And grave with wonder gazed about ;
85 The cock his lusty greeting said,
    And forth his speckled harem led ;
    The oxen lashed their tails, and hooked,
    And mild reproach of hunger looked ;
    The hornéd patriarch of the sheep,
90 Like Egypt's Amun roused from sleep,
    Shook his sage head with gesture mute,
    And emphasized with stamp of foot.

    All day the gusty north-wind bore
    The loosening drift its breath before ;
95 Low circling round its southern zone,
    The sun through dazzling snow-mist shone.
    No church-bell lent its Christian tone
    To the savage air, no social smoke
    Curled over woods of snow-hung oak.

90. *Amun*, or Ammon, was an Egyptian being, representing an attribute
of Deity under the form of a ram.

100 A solitude made more intense
By dreary-voicéd elements,
The shrieking of the mindless wind,
The moaning tree-boughs swaying blind,
And on the glass the unmeaning beat
105 Of ghostly finger-tips of sleet.
Beyond the circle of our hearth
No welcome sound of toil or mirth
Unbound the spell, and testified
Of human life and thought outside.
110 We minded that the sharpest ear
The buried brooklet could not hear,
The music of whose liquid lip
Had been to us companionship,
And, in our lonely life, had grown
115 To have an almost human tone.

As night drew on, and, from the crest
Of wooded knolls that ridged the west,
The sun, a snow-blown traveller, sank
From sight beneath the smothering bank,
120 We piled with care our nightly stack
Of wood against the chimney-back, —
The oaken log, green, huge, and thick,
And on its top the stout back-stick;
The knotty forestick laid apart,
125 And filled between with curious art
The ragged brush; then, hovering near,
We watched the first red blaze appear,
Heard the sharp crackle, caught the gleam
On whitewashed wall and sagging beam,
130 Until the old, rude-furnished room
Burst, flower-like, into rosy bloom;

While radiant with a mimic flame
Outside the sparkling drift became,
And through the bare-boughed lilac-tree
135 Our own warm hearth seemed blazing free.
The crane and pendent trammels showed,
The Turk's heads on the andirons glowed ;
While childish fancy, prompt to tell
The meaning of the miracle,
140 Whispered the old rhyme : " *Under the tree,*
When fire outdoors burns merrily,
There the witches are making tea."

The moon above the eastern wood
Shone at its full ; the hill-range stood
145 Transfigured in the silver flood,
Its blown snows flashing cold and keen,
Dead white, save where some sharp ravine
Took shadow. or the sombre green
Of hemlocks turned to pitchy black
150 Against the whiteness of their back.
For such a world and such a night
Most fitting that unwarming light,
Which only seemed where'er it fell
To make the coldness visible.

155 Shut in from all the world without,
We sat the clean-winged hearth about,
Content to let the north-wind roar
In battle rage at pane and door,
While the red logs before us beat
160 The frost-line back with tropic heat ;
And ever, when a louder blast
Shook beam and rafter as it passed,

The merrier up its roaring draught
The great throat of the chimney laughed,
165 The house-dog on his paws outspread
Laid to the fire his drowsy head,
The cat's dark silhouette on the wall
A couchant tiger's seemed to fall;
And, for the winter fireside meet,
170 Between the andirons' straddling feet,
The mug of cider simmered slow,
The apples sputtered in a row,
And, close at hand, the basket stood
With nuts from brown October's wood.

175 What matter how the night behaved?
What matter how the north-wind raved?
Blow high, blow low, not all its snow
Could quench our hearth-fire's ruddy glow.
O Time and Change! — with hair as gray
180 As was my sire's that winter day,
How strange it seems, with so much gone
Of life and love, to still live on!
Ah, brother! only I and thou
Are left of all that circle now, —
185 The dear home faces whereupon
That fitful firelight paled and shone.
Henceforward, listen as we will,
The voices of that hearth are still;
Look where we may, the wide earth o'er,
190 Those lighted faces smile no more.
We tread the paths their feet have worn,
  We sit beneath their orchard trees,
  We hear, like them, the hum of bees
And rustle of the bladed corn;

195 We turn the pages that they read,
    Their written words we linger o'er,
But in the sun they cast no shade,
No voice is heard, no sign is made,
    No step is on the conscious floor!

200 Yet Love will dream and Faith will trust
(Since He who knows our need is just)
That somehow, somewhere, meet we must.
Alas for him who never sees
The stars shine through his cypress-trees!

205 Who, hopeless, lays his dead away,
Nor looks to see the breaking day
Across the mournful marbles play!
Who hath not learned, in hours of faith,
    The truth to flesh and sense unknown,

210 That Life is ever lord of Death,
    And Love can never lose its own!

We sped the time with stories old,
Wrought puzzles out, and riddles told,
Or stammered from our school-book lore

215 "The chief of Gambia's golden shore."
How often since, when all the land
Was clay in Slavery's shaping hand,
As if a trumpet called, I've heard
Dame Mercy Warren's rousing word:

220 "*Does not the voice of reason cry,*
    Claim the first right which Nature gave,
From the red scourge of bondage fly,
    Nor deign to live a burdened slave!"

219. Mrs. Mercy Warren was the wife of James Warren, a prominent patriot at the beginning of the Revolution. Her poetry was read in an age that had in America little to read under that name; her society was sought by the best men.

Our father rode again his ride
225 On Memphremagog's wooded side ;
Sat down again to moose and samp
In trapper's hut and Indian camp ;
Lived o'er the old idyllic ease
Beneath St. François' hemlock-trees ;
230 Again for him the moonlight shone
On Norman cap and bodiced zone ;
Again he heard the violin play
Which led the village dance away,
And mingled in its merry whirl
235 The grandam and the laughing girl.
Or, nearer home, our steps he led
Where Salisbury's level marshes spread
Mile-wide as flies the laden bee ;
Where merry mowers, hale and strong,
240 Swept, scythe on scythe, their swaths along
The low green prairies of the sea.
We shared the fishing of Boar's Head,
And round the rocky Isles of Shoals
The hake-broil on the driftwood coals ;
245 The chowder on the sand-beach made,
Dipped by the hungry, steaming hot,
With spoons of clam-shell from the pot.
We heard the tales of witchcraft old,
And dream and sign and marvel told
250 To sleepy listeners as they lay
Stretched idly on the salted hay,
Adrift along the winding shores,
When favoring breezes deigned to blow
The square sail of the gundalow,
255 And idle lay the useless oars.

Our mother. while she turned her wheel
Or run the new-knit stocking-heel.
Told how the Indian hordes came down
At midnight on Cochecho town.
 And how her own great-uncle bore
His cruel scalp-mark to forescore.
Recalling. in her fitting phrase.
  So rich and picturesque and free
  (The common unrhymed poetry
 Of simple life and country ways(.
The story of her early days. —
She made us welcome to her home :
Old hearths grew wide to give us room :
We stole with her a frightened look
 At the gray wizard's conjuring-book.
The fame whereof went far and wide
Through all the simple country-side :
We heard the hawks at twilight play.
The boat-horn on Piscataqua.
 The loon's weird laughter far away ;
We fished her little trout-brook. knew
What flowers in wood and meadow grew.
What sunny hillsides autumn-brown
She climbed to shake the ripe nuts down.
 Saw where in sheltered cove and bay
The ducks' black squadron anchored lay.
And heard the wild geese calling loud
Beneath the gray November cloud.
Then. haply. with a book more grave.
 And soberer tone. some tale she gave
From painful Sewel's ancient tome.

Beloved in every Quaker home.
Of faith fire-winged by martyrdom,
Or Chalkley's Journal, old and quaint, —
290 Gentlest of skippers, rare sea-saint ! —
Who, when the dreary calms prevailed,
And water-butt and bread-cask failed,
And cruel, hungry eyes pursued
His portly presence, mad for food,
295 With dark hints muttered under breath
Of casting lots for life or death,
Offered, if Heaven withheld supplies,
To be himself the sacrifice.
Then, suddenly, as if to save
300 The good man from his living grave,

seemed to have as good an opinion of the book as Whittier. In his essay
A Quakers' Meeting in *Essays of Elia*, he says : "Reader, if you are not ac-
quainted with it, I would recommend to you, above all church-narratives, to
read Sewel's *History of the Quakers*. . . . It is far more edifying and affecting
than anything you will read of Wesley or his colleagues."

289. Thomas Chalkley was an Englishman of Quaker parentage, born in
1675, who travelled extensively as a preacher, and finally made his home in
Philadelphia. He died in 1749 ; his *Journal* was first published in 1747. His
own narrative of the incident which the poet relates is as follows : "To stop
their murmuring, I told them they should not need to cast lots, which was
usual in such cases, which of us should die first, for I would freely offer up my
life to do them good. One said, 'God bless you ! I will not eat any of you.'
Another said, 'He would die before he would eat any of me ;' and so said
several. I can truly say, on that occasion, at that time, my life was not dear
to me, and that I was serious and ingenuous in my proposition : and as I was
leaning over the side of the vessel, thoughtfully considering my proposal to
the company, and looking in my mind to Him that made me, a very large dol-
phin came up towards the top or surface of the water, and looked me in the
face ; and I called the people to put a hook into the sea, and take him, for
here is one come to redeem me (I said to them). And they put a hook into
the sea, and the fish readily took it, and they caught him. He was longer
than myself. I think he was about six feet long, and the largest that ever I
saw. This plainly showed us that we ought not to distrust the providence
of the Almighty. The people were quieted by this act of Providence, and
murmured no more. We caught enough to eat plentifully of, till we got into
the capes of Delaware."

A ripple on the water grew,
A school of porpoise flashed in view.
" Take, eat," he said, " and be content ;
These fishes in my stead are sent   ·
305 By Him who gave the tangled ram
To spare the child of Abraham."

Our uncle, innocent of books,
Was rich in lore of fields and brooks,
The ancient teachers never dumb
310 Of Nature's unhoused lyceum.
In moons and tides and weather wise,
He read the clouds as prophecies,
And foul or fair could well divine,
` By many an occult hint and sign,
315 Holding the cunning-warded keys
To all the woodcraft mysteries ;
Himself to Nature's heart so near
That all her voices in his ear
Of beast or bird had meanings clear,
320 Like Apollonius of old,   ·
Who knew the tales the sparrows told,
Or Hermes, who interpreted
What the sage cranes of Nilus said ;
A simple, guileless, childlike man,
325 Content to live where life began ;
Strong only on his native grounds,

310. The measure requires the accent ly'ceum, but in stricter use the accent
is lyce'um.

320. A philosopher born in the first century of the Christian era, of whom
many strange stories were told, especially regarding his converse with birds
and animals.

322. Hermes Trismegistus, a celebrated Egyptian priest and philosopher,
to whom was attributed the revival of geometry, arithmetic, and art among
the Egyptians.   He was little later than Apollonius.

The little world of sights and sounds
Whose girdle was the parish bounds,
Whereof his fondly partial pride
330 The common features magnified,
As Surrey hills to mountains grew
In White of Selborne's loving view, —
He told how teal and loon he shot,
And how the eagle's eggs he got,
335 The feats on pond and river done,
The prodigies of rod and gun ;
Till, warming with the tales he told,
Forgotten was the outside cold,
The bitter wind unheeded blew,
340 From ripening corn the pigeons flew,
The partridge drummed i' the wood, the mink
Went fishing down the river-brink.
In fields with bean or clover gay,
The woodchuck, like a hermit gray,
345 Peered from the doorway of his cell ;
The muskrat plied the mason's trade,
And tier by tier his mud-walls laid ;
And from the shagbark overhead
The grizzled squirrel dropped his shell.

350 Next, the dear aunt, whose smile of cheer
And voice in dreams I see and hear, —
The sweetest woman ever Fate
Perverse denied a household mate,
Who, lonely. homeless, not the less
355 Found peace in love's unselfishness,

332. Gilbert White, of Selborne, England, was a clergyman who wrote the *Natural History of Selborne*, a minute, affectionate, and charming description of what could be seen as it were from his own doorstep. The accuracy of his observation and the delightfulness of his manner have kept the book a classic.

And welcome whereso'er she went,
A calm and gracious element,
Whose presence seemed the sweet income
And womanly atmosphere of home, —
360 Called up her girlhood memories,
The huskings and the apple-bees,
The sleigh-rides and the summer sails,
Weaving through all the poor details
And homespun warp of circumstance
365 A golden woof-thread of romance.
For well she kept her genial mood
And simple faith of maidenhood;
Before her still a cloud-land lay,
The mirage loomed across her way;
370 The morning dew, that dried so soon
With others, glistened at her noon;
Through years of toil and soil and care,
From glossy tress to thin gray hair,
All unprofaned she held apart
375 The virgin fancies of the heart.
Be shame to him of woman born
Who had for such but thought of scorn.

There, too, our elder sister plied
Her evening task the stand beside;
380 A full, rich nature, free to trust,
Truthful and almost sternly just,
Impulsive, earnest, prompt to act,
And make her generous thought a fact,
Keeping with many a light disguise
385 The secret of self-sacrifice.
O heart sore-tried! thou hast the best
That Heaven itself could give thee, — rest,

Rest from all bitter thoughts and things !
How many a poor one's blessing went
390 With thee beneath the low green tent
Whose curtain never outward swings !

As one who held herself a part
Of all she saw, and let her heart
Against the household bosom lean,
395 Upon the motley-braided mat
Our youngest and our dearest sat,
Lifting her large, sweet, asking eyes,
Now bathed within the fadeless green
And holy peace of Paradise.
400 Oh, looking from some heavenly hill,
Or from the shade of saintly palms,
Or silver reach of river calms,
Do those large eyes behold me still ?
With me one little year ago : —
405 The chill weight of the winter snow
For months upon her grave has lain ;
And now, when summer south-winds blow
And brier and harebell bloom again,
I tread the pleasant paths we trod,
410 I see the violet-sprinkled sod,
Whereon she leaned, too frail and weak
The hillside flowers she loved to seek,
Yet following me where'er I went
With dark eyes full of love's content.
415 The birds are glad ; the brier-rose fills
The air with sweetness ; all the hills
Stretch green to June's unclouded sky ;

---

398. *Th' unfading green* would be harsher but more correct since the termination *less* is added to nouns and not to verbs.

But still I wait with ear and eye
For something gone which should be nigh,
420 A loss in all familiar things,
In flower that blooms, and bird that sings.
And yet, dear heart! remembering thee,
Am I not richer than of old?
Safe in thy immortality,
425   What change can reach the wealth I hold?
What chance can mar the pearl and gold
Thy love hath left in trust with me?
And while in life's late afternoon,
Where cool and long the shadows grow,
430 I walk to meet the night that soon
Shall shape and shadow overflow,
I cannot feel that thou art far,
Since near at need the angels are;
And when the sunset gates unbar,
435   Shall I not see thee waiting stand,
And, white against the evening star,
The welcome of thy beckoning hand?

Brisk wielder of the birch and rule,
The master of the district school
440 Held at the fire his favored place;
Its warm glow lit a laughing face
Fresh-hued and fair, where scarce appeared
The uncertain prophecy of beard.
He teased the mitten-blinded cat,
445 Played cross-pins on my uncle's hat,
Sang songs, and told us what befalls
In classic Dartmouth's college halls.
Born the wild Northern hills among,
From whence his yeoman father wrung

450 By patient toil subsistence scant,
Not competence and yet not want,
He early gained the power to pay
His cheerful, self-reliant way ;
Could doff at ease his scholar's gown
455 To peddle wares from town to town ;
Or through the long vacation's reach
In lonely lowland districts teach,
Where all the droll experience found
At stranger hearths in boarding round,
460 The moonlit skater's keen delight,
The sleigh-drive through the frosty night,
The rustic party, with its rough
Accompaniment of blind-man's-buff,
And whirling plate, and forfeits paid,
465 His winter task a pastime made.
Happy the snow-locked homes wherein
He tuned his merry violin,
Or played the athlete in the barn,
Or held the good dame's winding yarn,
470 Or mirth-provoking versions told
Of classic legends rare and old,
Wherein the scenes of Greece and Rome
Had all the commonplace of home,
And little seemed at best the odds
475 'Twixt Yankee pedlers and old gods ;
Where Pindus-born Araxes took
The guise of any grist-mill brook,
And dread Olympus at his will
Became a huckleberry hill.

---

476. Pindus is the mountain chain which, running from north to south,
nearly bisects Greece. Five rivers take their rise from the central peak, the
Aöus, the Arachthus, the Haliacmou, the Penëus, and the Achelöus.

430 A careless boy that night he seemed;
But at his desk he had the look
And air of one who wisely schemed,
And hostage from the future took
In trainèd thought and lore of book.

435 Large-brained, clear-eyed, — of such as he
Shall Freedom's young apostles be,
Who, following in War's bloody trail,
Shall every lingering wrong assail;
All chains from limb and spirit strike,

440 Uplift the black and white alike;
Scatter before their swift advance
The darkness and the ignorance,
The pride, the lust, the squalid sloth,
Which nurtured Treason's monstrous growth,

445 Made murder pastime, and the hell
Of prison-torture possible;
The cruel lie of caste refute,
Old forms remould, and substitute
For Slavery's lash the freeman's will,

500 For blind routine, wise-handed skill;
A school-house plant on every hill,
Stretching in radiate nerve-lines thence
The quick wires of intelligence;
Till North and South together brought

505 Shall own the same electric thought,
In peace a common flag salute,
And, side by side in labor's free
And unresentful rivalry,
Harvest the fields wherein they fought.

510 Another guest that winter night
Flashed back from lustrous eyes the light.

Unmarked by time, and yet not young,
The honeyed music of her tongue
And words of meekness scarcely told
515 A nature passionate and bold,
Strong, self-concentred, spurning guide,
Its milder features dwarfed beside
Her unbent will's majestic pride.
She sat among us, at the best,
520 A not unfeared, half-welcome guest,
Rebuking with her cultured phrase
Our homeliness of words and ways.
A certain pard-like, treacherous grace
Swayed the lithe limbs and dropped the lash,
525 Lent the white teeth their dazzling flash;
And under low brows, black with night,
Rayed out at times a dangerous light;
The sharp heat-lightnings of her face
Presaging ill to him whom Fate
530 Condemned to share her love or hate.
A woman tropical, intense
In thought and act, in soul and sense,
She blended in a like degree
The vixen and the devotee,
535 Revealing with each freak or feint
The temper of Petruchio's Kate,
The raptures of Siena's saint.
Her tapering hand and rounded wrist
Had facile power to form a fist;
540 The warm, dark languish of her eyes
Was never safe from wrath's surprise.

536. See Shakespeare's comedy of the *Taming of the Shrew.*
537. St. Catherine of Siena, who is represented as having wonderful visions. She made a vow of silence for three years.

Brows saintly calm and lips devout
Knew every change of scowl and pout;
And the sweet voice had notes more high
545 And shrill for social battle-cry.

Since then what old cathedral town
Has missed her pilgrim staff and gown,
What convent-gate has held its lock
Against the challenge of her knock!

550 Through Smyrna's plague-hushed thoroughfares,
Up sea-set Malta's rocky stairs,
Gray olive slopes of hills that hem
Thy tombs and shrines, Jerusalem,
Or startling on her desert throne
555 The crazy Queen of Lebanon
With claims fantastic as her own,
Her tireless feet have held their way;
And still, unrestful, bowed, and gray,
She watches under Eastern skies,
560 With hope each day renewed and fresh,
The Lord's quick coming in the flesh,
Whereof she dreams and prophesies!

Where'er her troubled path may be,
The Lord's sweet pity with her go!

555. An interesting account of Lady Hester Stanhope, an English gentle-woman who led a singular life on Mount Lebanon in Syria, will be found in Kinglake's *Eothen*, chapter viii.

562. This *not un-feared, half-welcome guest* was Miss Harriet Livermore, daughter of Judge Livermore of New Hampshire. She was a woman of fine powers, but wayward, wild, and enthusiastic. She went on an independent mission to the Western Indians, whom she, in common with some others, believed to be remnants of the lost tribes of Israel. At the time of this narrative she was about twenty-eight years old, but much of her life afterward was spent in the Orient. She was at one time the companion and friend of Lady Hester Stanhope, but finally quarreled with her about the use of the holy horses kept in the stable in waiting for the Lord's ride to Jerusalem at the second advent.

565 The outward wayward life we see,
    The hidden springs we may not know.
  Nor is it given us to discern
    What threads the fatal sisters spun,
    Through what ancestral years has run
570 The sorrow with the woman born,
    What forged her cruel chain of moods,
    What set her feet in solitudes,
      And held the love within her mute,
    What mingled madness in the blood,
575   A lifelong discord and annoy,
      Water of tears with oil of joy,
    And hid within the folded bud
      Perversities of flower and fruit.
    It is not ours to separate
580 The tangled skein of will and fate,
    To show what metes and bounds should stand
    Upon the soul's debatable land,
    And between choice and Providence
    Divide the circle of events;
585   But He who knows our frame is just,
    Merciful and compassionate,
    And full of sweet assurances
    And hope for all the language is,
      That He remembereth we are dust!

590 At last the great logs, crumbling low,
    Sent out a dull and duller glow,
    The bull's-eye watch that hung in view,
    Ticking its weary circuit through,
    Pointed with mutely-warning sign
595 Its black hand to the hour of nine.
    That sign the pleasant circle broke:

My uncle ceased his pipe to smoke,
Knocked from its bowl the refuse gray,
And laid it tenderly away,
600 Then roused himself to safely cover
The dull red brand with ashes over.
And while, with care, our mother laid
The work aside, her steps she stayed
One moment, seeking to express
605 Her grateful sense of happiness
For food and shelter, warmth and health,
And love's contentment more than wealth,
With simple wishes (not the weak,
Vain prayers which no fulfilment seek,
610 But such as warm the generous heart,
O'er-prompt to do with Heaven its part)
That none might lack, that bitter night,
For bread and clothing, warmth and light.

Within our beds awhile we heard
615 The wind that round the gables roared,
With now and then a ruder shock,
Which made our very bedsteads rock.
We heard the loosened clapboards tost,
The board-nails snapping in the frost;
620 And on us, through the unplastered wall,
Felt the lightsifted snow-flakes fall,
But sleep stole on, as sleep will do
When hearts are light and life is new;
Faint and more faint the murmurs grew,
625 Till in the summer-land of dreams
They softened to the sound of streams,
Low stir of leaves, and dip of oars,
And lapsing waves on quiet shores.

Next morn we wakened with the shout
630 Of merry voices high and clear;
 And saw the teamsters drawing near
 To break the drifted highways out.
 Down the long hillside treading slow
 We saw the half-buried oxen go,
635 Shaking the snow from heads uptost,
 Their straining nostrils white with frost.
 Before our door the straggling train
 Drew up, an added team to gain.
 The elders threshed their hands a-cold,
640 Passed, with the cider-mug, their jokes
  From lip to lip; the younger folks
 Down the loose snow-banks, wrestling, rolled,
 Then toiled again the cavalcade
  O'er windy hill, through clogged ravine,
645 And woodland paths that wound between
 Low drooping pine-boughs winter-weighed.
 From every barn a team afoot,
 At every house a new recruit,
 Where, drawn by Nature's subtlest law,
650 Haply the watchful young men saw
 Sweet doorway pictures of the curls
 And curious eyes of merry girls,
 Lifting their hands in mock defence
 Against the snow-balls' compliments,
655 And reading in each missive tost
 The charm which Eden never lost.

We heard once more the sleigh-bells' sound;
And, following where the teamsters led,
The wise old Doctor went his round,

---

659. The *wise old Doctor* was Dr. Weld of Haverhill, an able man, who died
at the age of ninety-six.

660 Just pausing at our door to say,
In the brief autocratic way
Of one who, prompt at Duty's call,
Was free to urge her claim on all,
That some poor neighbor sick abed
665 At night our mother's aid would need.
For, one in generous thought and deed,
What mattered in the sufferer's sight
The Quaker matron's inward light,
The Doctor's mail of Calvin's creed?
670 All hearts confess the saints elect
Who, twain in faith, in love agree,
And melt not in an acid sect
The Christian pearl of charity!

So days went on: a week had passed
675 Since the great world was heard from last.
The Almanac we studied o'er,
Read and reread our little store
Of books and pamphlets, scarce a score;
One harmless novel, mostly hid
680 From younger eyes, a book forbid,
And poetry, (or good or bad,
A single book was all we had.)
Where Ellwood's meek, drab-skirted Muse,
A stranger to the heathen Nine,
685 Sang, with a somewhat nasal whine,
The wars of David and the Jews.

683. Thomas Ellwood, one of the Society of Friends, a contemporary and friend of Milton, and the suggestor of *Paradise Regained*, wrote an epic poem in five books, called *Davideis*, the life of King David of Israel. He wrote the book, we are told, for his own diversion, so it was not necessary that others should be diverted by it. Ellwood's autobiography, a quaint and delightful book, has recently been issued in Howells's series of *Choice Autobiography*.

At last the floundering carrier bore
The village paper to our door.

Lo! broadening outward as we read,
690 To warmer zones the horizon spread;
In panoramic length unrolled
We saw the marvels that it told.
Before us passed the painted Creeks,
    And daft McGregor on his raids
695   In Costa Rica's everglades.

And up Taygetus winding slow
Rode Ypsilanti's Mainote Greeks,
A Turk's head at each saddle bow!
Welcome to us its week-old news,
700 Its corner for the rustic Muse,
    Its monthly gauge of snow and rain,
Its record, mingling in a breath
The wedding knell and dirge of death;
Jest, anecdote, and love-lorn tale,
705 The latest culprit sent to jail;
Its hue and cry of stolen and lost,
Its vendue sales and goods at cost,
    And traffic calling loud for gain.
We felt the stir of hall and street,
710 The pulse of life that round us beat;
The chill embargo of the snow
Was melted in the genial glow;
Wide swung again our ice-locked door,
And all the world was ours once more!

693. Referring to the removal of the Creek Indians from Georgia to beyond the Mississippi.

694. In 1822 Sir Gregor McGregor, a Scotchman, began an ineffectual attempt to establish a colony in Costa Rica.

697. Taygetus is a mountain on the Gulf of Messenia in Greece, and near by is the district of Maina, noted for its robbers and pirates. It was from these mountaineers that Ypsilanti, a Greek patriot, drew his cavalry in the struggle with Turkey which resulted in the independence of Greece.

715 Clasp, Angel of the backward look
And folded wings of ashen gray
And voice of echoes far away,
The brazen covers of thy book ;
The weird palimpsest old and vast,
720 Wherein thou hid'st the spectral past ;
Where, closely mingling, pale and glow
The characters of joy and woe ;
The monographs of outlived years,
Or smile-illumed or dim with tears,
725   Green hills of life that slope to death,
And haunts of home, whose vistaed trees
Shade off to mournful cypresses
    With the white amaranths underneath.
Even while I look, I can but heed
730   The restless sands' incessant fall,
Importunate hours that hours succeed,
Each clamorous with its own sharp need,
And duty keeping pace with all.
Shut down and clasp the heavy lids ;
735 I hear again the voice that bids
The dreamer leave his dream midway
For larger hopes and graver fears :
Life greatens in these later years,
The century's aloe flowers to-day !

740 Yet, haply, in some lull of life,
Some Truce of God which breaks its strife,

741. The name is drawn from a historic compact in 1040, when the Church forbade the barons to make any attack on each other between sunset on Wednesday and sunrise on the following Monday, or upon any ecclesiastical fast or feast day. It also provided that no man was to molest a laborer work-ing in the fields, or to lay hands on any implement of husbandry, on pain of excommunication.

The worldling's eyes shall gather dew,
  Dreaming in throngful city ways
Of winter joys his boyhood knew ;
745 And dear and early friends — the few
  Who yet remain — shall pause to view
    These Flemish pictures of old days ;
Sit with me by the homestead hearth,
And stretch the hands of memory forth
750   To warm them at the wood-fire's blaze !
And thanks untraced to lips unknown
Shall greet me like the odors blown
From unseen meadows newly mown,
Or lilies floating in some pond,
755 Wood-fringed, the wayside gaze beyond ;
The traveller owns the grateful sense
Of sweetness near, he knows not whence,
And, pausing, takes with forehead bare
The benediction of the air.

747. The Flemish school of painting was chiefly occupied with homely interiors.

II.

AMONG THE HILLS.

PRELUDE.

ALONG the roadside, like the flowers of gold
That tawny Incas for their gardens wrought,
Heavy with sunshine droops the golden-rod,
And the red pennons of the cardinal-flowers
5 Hang motionless upon their upright staves.
The sky is hot and hazy, and the wind,
Wing-weary with its long flight from the south,
Unfelt; yet, closely scanned, yon maple leaf
With faintest motion, as one stirs in dreams,
10 Confesses it. The locust by the wall
Stabs the noon-silence with his sharp alarm.
A single hay-cart down the dusty road
Creaks slowly, with its driver fast asleep
On the load's top. Against the neighboring hill,
15 Huddled along the stone wall's shady side,
The sheep show white, as if a snowdrift still
Defied the dog-star. Through the open door
A drowsy smell of flowers — gray heliotrope,
And white sweet clover, and shy mignonette —
20 Comes faintly in, and silent chorus lends
To the pervading symphony of peace.

2. The Incas were the kings of the ancient Peruvians. At Yucay, their
favorite residence, the gardens, according to Prescott, contained "forms of
vegetable life skillfully imitated in gold and silver." See *History of the Con-
quest of Peru*, i. 130.

No time is this for hands long over-worn
To task their strength: and (unto Him be praise
Who giveth quietness!) the stress and strain
25 Of years that did the work of centuries
Have ceased, and we can draw our breath once more
Freely and full. So, as you harvesters
Make glad their nooning underneath the elms
With tale and riddle and old snatch of song,
30 I lay aside grave themes, and idly turn
The leaves of memory's sketch-book, dreaming o'er
Old summer pictures of the quiet hills,
And human life, as quiet, at their feet.

And yet not idly all. A farmer's son,
35 Proud of field-lore and harvest craft ; and feeling
All their fine possibilities, how rich
And restful even poverty and toil
Become when beauty, harmony, and love
Sit at their humble hearth as angels sat
40 At evening in the patriarch's tent, when man
Makes labor noble, and his farmer's frock
The symbol of a Christian chivalry,
Tender and just and generous to her
Who clothes with grace all duty ; still, I know
45 Too well the picture has another side.
How wearily the grind of toil goes on
Where love is wanting, how the eye and ear
And heart are starved amidst the plenitude
Of nature, and how hard and colorless
50 Is life without an atmosphere. I look
Across the lapse of half a century,
And call to mind old homesteads, where no flower

26. The volume in which this poem stands first, and to which it gives the
name, was published in the fall of 1868.

Told that the spring had come, but evil weeds,
Nightshade and rough-leaved burdock, in the place
55 Of the sweet doorway greeting of the rose
And honeysuckle, where the house walls seemed
Blistering in sun, without a tree or vine
To cast the tremulous shadow of its leaves
Across the curtainless windows from whose panes
60 Fluttered the signal rags of shiftlessness ;
Within, the cluttered kitchen floor, unwashed
(Broom-clean I think they called it) ; the best room
Stifling with cellar damp, shut from the air
In hot midsummer, bookless, pictureless
65 Save the inevitable sampler hung
Over the fireplace, or a mourning piece,
A green-haired woman, peony-cheeked, beneath
Impossible willows ; the wide-throated hearth
Bristling with faded pine-boughs half concealing
70 The piled-up rubbish at the chimney's back ;
And, in sad keeping with all things about them,
Shrill, querulous women, sour and sullen men,
Untidy, loveless, old before their time,
With scarce a human interest save their own
75 Monotonous round of small economies,
Or the poor scandal of the neighborhood ;
Blind to the beauty everywhere revealed;
Treading the May-flowers with regardless feet ;
For them the song-sparrow and the bobolink
80 Sang not, nor winds made music in the leaves ;
For them in vain October's holocaust
Burned, gold and crimson, over all the hills,
The sacramental mystery of the woods.
Church-goers, fearful of the unseen Powers,
82 But grumbling over pulpit-tax and pew-rent,

Saving, as shrewd economists, their souls
And winter pork with the least possible outlay
Of salt and sanctity ; in daily life
Showing as little actual comprehension
90 Of Christian charity and love and duty,
As if the Sermon on the Mount had been
Outdated like a last year's almanac :
Rich in broad woodlands and in half-tilled fields,
And yet so pinched and bare and comfortless,
95 The veriest straggler limping on his rounds,
The sun and air his sole inheritance,
Laughed at poverty that paid its taxes,
And hugged his rags in self-complacency !

Not such should be the homesteads of a land
100 Where whoso wisely wills and acts may dwell
As king and lawgiver, in broad-acred state,
With beauty, art, taste, culture, books, to make
His hour of leisure richer than a life
Of fourscore to the barons of old time,
105 Our yeoman should be equal to his home,
Set in the fair, green valleys. purple walled,
A man to match his mountains, not to creep
Dwarfed and abased below them.   I would fain
In this light way (of which I needs must own
110 With the knife-grinder of whom Canning sings,
" Story, God bless you ! I have none to tell you ! ")
Invite the eye to see and heart to feel

110. The *Anti-Jacobin* was a periodical published in England in 1797-98, to ridicule democratic opinions, and in it Canning, who afterward became premier of England, wrote many light verses and *jeux d'esprit*, among them a humorous poem called the *Needy Knife-Grinder*, in burlesque of a poem by Southey. The knife-grinder is anxiously appealed to to tell his story of wrong and injustice, but answers as here : —

"Story, God bless you ! I've none to tell."

The beauty and the joy within their reach, —
Home, and home loves, and the beatitudes
115 Of nature free to all. Haply in years
That wait to take the places of our own,
Heard where some breezy balcony looks down
On happy homes, or where the lake in the moon
Sleeps dreaming of the mountains, fair as Ruth,
120 In the old Hebrew pastoral, at the feet
Of Boaz, even this simple lay of mine
May seem the burden of a prophecy,
Finding its late fulfilment in a change
Slow as the oak's growth, lifting manhood up
125 Through broader culture, finer manners, love,
And reverence, to the level of the hills.

O Golden Age, whose light is of the dawn,
And not of sunset, forward, not behind,
Flood the new heavens and earth, and with thee
bring
130 All the old virtues, whatsoever things
Are pure and honest and of good repute,
But add thereto whatever bard has sung
Or seer has told of when in trance and dream
They saw the Happy Isles of prophecy!
135 Let Justice hold her scale, and Truth divide
Between the right and wrong; but give the heart
The freedom of its fair inheritance;
Let the poor prisoner, cramped and starved so
long,
At Nature's table feast his ear and eye

---

134. The Fortunate Isles, or Isles of the Blest, were imaginary islands in
the West, in classic mythology, set in a sea which was warmed by the rays of
the declining sun. Hither the favorites of the gods were borne and dwelt in
endless joy.

140 With joy and wonder; let all harmonies
　　Of sound, form, color, motion, wait upon
　　The princely guest, whether in soft attire
　　Of leisure clad, or the coarse frock of toil,
　　And, lending life to the dead form of faith,
145 Give human nature reverence for the sake
　　Of One who bore it, making it divine
　　With the ineffable tenderness of God ;
　　Let common need, the brotherhood of prayer,
　　The heirship of an unknown destiny,
150 The unsolved mystery round about us, make
　　A man more precious than the gold of Ophir.
　　Sacred, inviolate, unto whom all things
　　Should minister, as outward types and signs
　　Of the eternal beauty which fulfils
155 The one great purpose of creation, Love,
　　The sole necessity of Earth and Heaven !

AMONG THE HILLS.

For weeks the clouds had raked the hills
　　And vexed the vales with raining,
And all the woods were sad with mist,
160 　And all the brooks complaining.

At last, a sudden night-storm tore
　　The mountain veils asunder,
And swept the valleys clean before
　　The besom of the thunder.

165 Through Sandwich notch the west-wind sang
　　Good morrow to the cotter ;

165. Sandwich Notch, Chocorua Mountain, Ossipee Lake, and the Bearcamp
River are all striking features of the scenery in that part of New Hampshire

And once again Chocorua's horn
Of shadow pierced the water.

Above his broad lake Ossipee,
170   Once more the sunshine wearing,
Stooped, tracing on that silver shield
His grim armorial bearing.

Clear drawn against the hard blue sky
The peaks had winter's keenness;
175 And, close on autumn's frost, the vales
Had more than June's fresh greenness.

Again the sodden forest floors
With golden lights were checkered,
Once more rejoicing leaves in wind
180   And sunshine danced and flickered.

It was as if the summer's late
Atoning for its sadness
Had borrowed every season's charm
To end its days in gladness.

185 I call to mind those banded vales
Of shadow and of shining,
Through which, my hostess at my side,
I drove in day's declining.

We held our sideling way above
190   The river's whitening shallows,

which lies just at the entrance of the White Mountain region. Many of
Whittier's most graceful poems are drawn from the suggestions of this country,
where he has been wont to spend his summer months of late, and a mountain
near West Ossipee has received his name

By homesteads old, with wide-flung barns
    Swept through and through by swallows, —

By maple orchards, belts of pine
    And larches climbing darkly
195 The mountain slopes, and, over all,
    The great peaks rising starkly.

You should have seen that long hill-range
    With gaps of brightness riven, —
How through each pass and hollow streamed
200   The purpling lights of heaven, —

Rivers of gold-mist flowing down
    From far celestial fountains, —
The great sun flaming through the rifts
    Beyond the wall of mountains!

205 We paused at last where home-bound cows
    Brought down the pasture's treasure,
And in the barn the rhythmic flails
    Beat out a harvest measure.

We heard the night hawk's sullen plunge,
210   The crow his tree-mates calling:
The shadows lengthening down the slopes
    About our feet were falling,

And through them smote the level sun
    In broken lines of splendor,
215 Touched the gray rocks and made the green
    Of the shorn grass more tender.

The maples bending o'er the gate,
   Their arch of leaves just tinted
With yellow warmth, the golden glow
220   Of coming autumn hinted.

Keen white between the farm-house showed,
   And smiled on porch and trellis
The fair democracy of flowers
   That equals cot and palace.

225 And weaving garlands for her dog,
   'Twixt chidings and caresses,
A human flower of childhood shook
   The sunshine from her tresses.

On either hand we saw the signs
230   Of fancy and of shrewdness,
Where taste had wound its arms of vines
   Round thrift's uncomely rudeness.

The sun-brown farmer in his frock
   Shook hands, and called to Mary:
235 Bare-armed, as Juno might, she came,
   White-aproned from her dairy.

Her air, her smile, her motions, told
   Of womanly completeness;
A music as of household songs
240   Was in her voice of sweetness.

Not beautiful in curve and line,
   But something more and better,

The secret charm eluding art,
　　Its spirit, not its letter ; —

245 An inborn grace that nothing lacked
　　Of culture or appliance. —
　The warmth of genial courtesy,
　　The calm of self-reliance.

Before her queenly womanhood
250　　How dared our hostess utter
　The paltry errand of her need
　　To buy her fresh-churned butter ?

She led the way with housewife pride,
　　Her goodly store disclosing,
255 Full tenderly the golden balls
　　With practised hands disposing.

Then, while along the western hills
　　We watched the changeful glory
Of sunset, on our homeward way,
260　　I heard her simple story.

The early crickets sang ; the stream
　　Plashed through my friend's narration :
Her rustic patois of the hills
　　Lost in my free translation.

265 " More wise," she said, "than those who swarm
　　Our hills in middle summer,
She came, when June's first roses blow,
　　To greet the early comer.

" From school and ball and rout she came,
270   The city's fair, pale daughter,
To drink the wine of mountain air
Beside the Bearcamp Water.

" Her step grew firmer on the hills
That watch our homesteads over ;
275 On cheek and lip, from summer fields,
She caught the bloom of clover.

" For health comes sparkling in the streams
From cool Chocorua stealing :
There's iron in our Northern winds ;
280   Our pines are trees of healing.

" She sat beneath the broad-armed elms
That skirt the mowing-meadow,
And watched the gentle west-wind weave
The grass with shine and shadow.

285 " Beside her, from the summer heat
To share her grateful screening,
With forehead bared, the farmer stood,
Upon his pitchfork leaning.

" Framed in its damp, dark locks, his face
290   Had nothing mean or common, —
Strong, manly, true, the tenderness
And pride beloved of woman.

" She looked up, glowing with the health
The country air had brought her,

295 And. laughing, said : ' You lack a wife,
    Your mother lacks a daughter.

    " ' To mend your frock and bake your bread
      You do not need a lady :
  Be sure among these brown old homes
300   Is some one waiting ready, —

    " ' Some fair, sweet girl, with skilful hand
      And cheerful heart for treasure,
  Who never played with ivory keys,
    Or danced the polka's measure.'

305 " He bent his black brows to a frown,
    He set his white teeth tightly.
  ' 'T is well,' he said, ' for one like you
    To choose for me so lightly.

  " ' You think, because my life is rude
310   I take no note of sweetness :
  I tell you love has naught to do
    With meetness or unmeetness.

    " ' Itself its best excuse, it asks
      No leave of pride or fashion
315 When silken zone or homespun frock
    It stirs with throbs of passion.

    " ' You think me deaf and blind : you bring
      Your winning graces hither
  As free as if from cradle-time
320   We two had played together.

" 'You tempt me with your laughing eyes,
　　Your cheek of sundown's blushes,
　A motion as of waving grain,
　　A music as of thrushes.

325 " 'The plaything of your summer sport,
　　The spells you weave around me
　You cannot at your will undo,
　　Nor leave me as you found me.

" 'You go as lightly as you came,
330　　Your life is well without me ;
　What care you that these hills will close
　　Like prison-walls about me ?

" 'No mood is mine to seek a wife,
　　Or daughter for my mother :
335 Who loves you loses in that love
　　All power to love another !

" 'I dare your pity or your scorn,
　　With pride your own exceeding ;
　I fling my heart into your lap
340　　Without a word of pleading.'

" She looked up in his face of pain
　　So archly, yet so tender :
　'And if I lend you mine,' she said,
　　'Will you forgive the lender ?

345 " 'Nor frock nor tan can hide the man ;
　　And see you not, my farmer,

How weak and fond a woman waits
Behind this silken armor?

" ' I love you : on that love alone,
350   And not my worth, presuming,
Will you not trust for summer fruit
The tree in May-day blooming? '

" Alone the hangbird overhead,
His hair-swung cradle straining,
355 Looked down to see love's miracle, —
The giving that is gaining.

" And so the farmer found a wife,
His mother found a daughter:
There looks no happier home than hers
360   On pleasant Bearcamp Water.

" Flowers spring to blossom where she walks
The careful ways of duty;
Our hard, stiff lines of life with her
Are flowing curves of beauty.

365 " Our homes are cheerier for her sake,
Our door-yards brighter blooming,
And all about the social air
Is sweeter for her coming.

" Unspoken homilies of peace
370   Her daily life is preaching;
The still refreshment of the dew
Is her unconscious teaching.

"And never tenderer hand than hers
    Unknits the brow of ailing;
375 Her garments to the sick man's ear
    Have music in their trailing.

"And when, in pleasant harvest moons,
    The youthful huskers gather,
Or sleigh-drives on the mountain ways
380   Defy the winter weather, —

"In sugar-camps, when south and warm
    The winds of March are blowing,
And sweetly from its thawing veins
    The maple's blood is flowing, —

385 "In summer, where some lilied pond
    Its virgin zone is bearing,
Or where the ruddy autumn fire
    Lights up the apple-paring, —

"The coarseness of a ruder time
390   Her finer mirth displaces,
A subtler sense of pleasure fills
    Each rustic sport she graces.

"Her presence lends its warmth and health
    To all who come before it.
395 If woman lost us Eden, such
    As she alone restore it.

"For larger life and wiser aims
    The farmer is her debtor;

Who holds to his another's heart
400   Must needs be worse or better.

"Through her his civic service shows
    A purer-toned ambition ;
No double consciousness divides
    The man and politician.

405 "In party's doubtful ways he trusts
    Her instincts to determine ;
At the loud polls, the thought of her
    Recalls Christ's Mountain Sermon.

"He owns her logic of the heart,
410   And wisdom of unreason,
Supplying, while he doubts and weighs,
    The needed word in season.

"He sees with pride her richer thought,
    Her fancy's freer ranges ;
415 And love thus deepened to respect
    Is proof against all changes.

"And if she walks at ease in ways
    His feet are slow to travel,
And if she reads with cultured eyes
420   What his may scarce unravel,

"Still clearer, for her keener sight
    Of beauty and of wonder,
He learns the meaning of the hills
    He dwelt from childhood under.

425 " And higher, warmed with summer lights,
    Or winter-crowned and hoary,
The ridged horizon lifts for him
    Its inner veils of glory.

" He has his own free, bookless lore,
430   The lessons nature taught him,
The wisdom which the woods and hills
    And toiling men have brought him :

" The steady force of will whereby
    Her flexile grace seems sweeter ;
435 The sturdy counterpoise which makes
    Her woman's life completer :

" A latent fire of soul which lacks
    No breath of love to fan it ;
And wit, that, like his native brooks,
440   Plays over solid granite.

" How dwarfed against his manliness
    She sees the poor pretension,
The wants, the aims, the follies, born
    Of fashion and convention !

445 " How life behind its accidents
    Stands strong and self-sustaining,
The human fact transcending all
    The losing and the gaining.

" And so, in grateful interchange
    Of teacher and of hearer,

Their lives their true distinctness keep
  While daily drawing nearer.

" And if the husband or the wife
  In home's strong light discovers
455 Such slight defaults as failed to meet
  The blinded eyes of lovers,

" Why need we care to ask ? — who dreams
  Without their thorns of roses,
Or wonders that the truest steel
460 The readiest spark discloses ?

" For still in mutual sufferance lies
  The secret of true living :
Love scarce is love that never knows
  The sweetness of forgiving.

465 " We send the Squire to General Court,
  He takes his young wife thither ;
No prouder man election day
  Rides through the sweet June weather.

" He sees with eyes of manly trust
470 All hearts to her inclining ;
Not less for him his household light
  That others share its shining."

Thus, while my hostess spake, there grew
  Before me, warmer tinted

475 And outlined with a tenderer grace,
  The picture that she hinted.

The sunset smouldered as we drove
   Beneath the deep hill-shadows.
Below us wreaths of white fog walked
480   Like ghosts the haunted meadows.

Sounding the summer night, the stars
   Dropped down their golden plummets;
The pale arc of the Northern lights
   Rose o'er the mountain summits, —

485 Until, at last, beneath its bridge,
   We heard the Bearcamp flowing,
And saw across the mapled lawn
   The welcome home-lights glowing; —

And, musing on the tale I heard,
490   'T were well, thought I, if often
To rugged farm-life came the gift
   To harmonize and soften; —

If more and more we found the troth
   Of fact and fancy plighted,
495 And culture's charm and labor's strength
   In rural homes united, —

The simple life, the homely hearth,
   With beauty's sphere surrounding,
And blessing toil where toil abounds
500   With graces more abounding.